W9-AWD-780

Also by Leslie McGuirk

TUCKER FLIPS!
TUCKER OFF HIS ROCKER

TUCKER OVER THE TOP

Leslie McGuirk

Dutton Children's Books · New York

CIP Data is available.

Published in the United States 2000 by Dutton Children's Books,
a division of Penguin Putnam Books for Young Readers
345 Hudson Street, New York, New York 10014
www.penguinputnam.com
First Edition   Printed in Hong Kong
ISBN 0-525-46465-4
1 2 3 4 5 6 7 8 9 10

My nieces and nephews used to scream, "Tucker's under the table!" every time they ate popcorn, and he'd wait below, knowing they'd drop some. I dedicate this Tucker book to my two-fisted-popcorn-eating nieces and nephews—Chris, Mike, Marie, Lizzie, Donna, Hugh, Malcolm, and Emma!

Tucker watched sadly as his girl went off to a party. Dogs weren't invited.

She had promised to be back soon,
but what would he do until then?

He blew on a dandelion puff, wishing for adventure.
The seeds floated away on the breeze.

He hopped on his skateboard and followed them.

The seeds swirled toward a circus...

and one of his most favorite, delicious smells!

He took a spin past the jugglers

and scooted under the tigers on the trapeze.

He weaved between the hippos

and barked at a fierce lion.

He skated past the Flying Poodle Family,
then stopped short. *There* was the smell!

The head poodle had been watching Tucker.
"We could use you in our act," she said.

"All you have to do is skate down a ramp and make a jump. If you do a good job, you'll get all the popcorn you can eat."

Grrr

Tucker's stomach told him to say "YES."

But first he had to try on costumes!

He felt like a poodle, but he did it for the popcorn.

Then he saw what he had to jump over—

a HUGE elephant!

But it was too late to back out now.
The ringmaster gave him a push.

At the end of the ramp, Tucker flew into the air,

over the elephant, and...

into a giant tub of popcorn.

He smiled for the cameras.

He took his time getting out.

Then he bowed and bow-wowed.

"You're a superstar!" said the poodle. "How about flying with us again in our next show?"

Tucker shook his head as he climbed
out of his costume.
It was itchy around his neck.

Before the poodle could say another word,
Tucker was off on his skateboard again.

Tucker got home right before his girl did.
He lapped up lots of water.
The popcorn had made him thirsty.

"Tucker, I missed you!" she said.
"I brought you a special treat."

"It's your favorite—popcorn!"